OWEN FOOTE, SOCCER STAR

OWEN FOOTE, SOCCER STAR

by Stephanie Greene
illustrated by Martha Weston

SCHOLASTIC INC.

New York Toronto London Auckland Sydney
Mexico City New Delhi Hong Kong Buenos Aires

ISBN   0-439-57089-1

12 11 10 9 8 7 6 5 4 3   4 5 6 7 8/0

Printed in the U.S.A.   40

First Scholastic printing, October 2003

The illustrations were executed in pencil and ink wash.

For George
—S. G.

For Betsy, a loyal friend
—M. W.

CONTENTS

1.

THE GREATEST SPORT IN THE WORLD

"I am *somebody*!"

Owen leaped off his bed and landed in a crouched position in front of his mirror.

He squinted his eyes and stared at his reflection. First the left profile. Then the right.

He made a serious face. Then his bad guy face. There was no doubt about it.

"I'm the coolest guy in the whole wide world," he sang. He moved his skinny shoulders up and down like a rock star. He shuffled his feet in time to the music.

It was Friday afternoon. Owen's bed was

covered with books. There was a field guide to North American fishes and dolphins. A guide to amphibians and reptiles. Another one to birds.

Plus a whole bunch of other books about animals.

Owen loved to read about animals. He loved to read about how fast they could run. About what kinds of other animals they killed. How ferocious they were.

All this week he had been reading a book about gorillas. He thought gorillas were the greatest.

They were the largest and most powerful of all living primates, the book said. But they were very peaceful.

They lived in families. Their leader was called a silverback. No one bothered the silverback. He was so strong, he could tear a leopard apart with his bare hands.

The thought of it made Owen shiver.

The book said all the little gorillas respected

the silverback. They would do anything to be near him.

Every morning after the silverback got out of his bed, they got in it and rolled around. Having his smell on them made them feel strong. And proud.

Like they were somebody, the book said.

Owen knew just how they felt. He felt the same way about soccer. Just putting on his cleats made him feel ten feet tall. Or his shin guards. Or his shirt with the number 9 on the back.

It wasn't exactly the same, but it was pretty close.

He drummed his fists on his chest. "I am *somebody*!" he yelled again.

His sister Lydia opened his door.

"Hey, somebody," she said, "somebody wants you on the phone."

Owen took the stairs two at a time. He wished there was a vine so he could swing down.

"Hello?"

"It's Joseph. My mother got me those things you wear to protect your legs."

"Shin guards," Owen said. "Did you get cleats?"

"Yeah. It feels kind of funny, walking in them."

"Don't worry," Owen said. "You'll get used to it."

Joseph was Owen's best friend. They had been best friends since kindergarten. Joseph was big and Owen was small. They looked kind of funny, side by side. But that's the way they usually were. Because they liked to do everything together.

Like fish. And read. And build things.

Everything but play soccer. Joseph had never played. This was going to be his first time. It had taken Owen all summer to talk him into it.

"It's the greatest sport in the world," he told Joseph. "All you have to do is run and kick."

"Great," Joseph said in a gloomy voice. "The two things I can't do. Remember the Presidential Fitness Test?"

Owen did. Joseph had done almost as badly as Claire Price.

Claire Price was a chubby girl in their class who didn't run the mile run. She walked it. Even walking, the inside tops of her legs rubbed together. Her shorts pulled up. Her face got red and sweaty.

Claire Price came in last.

Joseph beat her. But not by that much.

"What if everyone laughs at me?" Joseph said.

"They won't," said Owen. "Everyone's the same. We'll be together. I'll protect you, Joseph, I promise." Joseph had finally agreed. But right now, he didn't sound too happy about it.

"Don't worry, Joseph, it's going to be great," Owen said. He didn't have to see Joseph's face to know what it looked like. Joseph could look worried better than anyone Owen knew. His eyebrows rose up in the middle. Like a mountain. His brown eyes turned black.

Even his eyeballs looked worried.

Owen couldn't imagine how anyone could be nervous about soccer. He had started playing in kindergarten. They played on the playground at Chesterfield School. All the kids knew one another. Everybody got to play. The coaches were fathers in real life.

This year, it was going to be different.

This year, they were in second grade. Second

grade was when you joined the town league. It had kids from other schools. The coaches had played soccer in college.

Best of all, they were going to play on a real soccer field. Owen's mom had driven him by. It had goals at either end and lines drawn all over it.

To Owen, it looked as long and wide as the ocean. It made him think of Pele, the world's most famous soccer player.

Owen had read all about Pele.

He was small, like Owen. But it didn't matter. He could jump higher than people's heads. He ran like the wind.

One look at that field and Owen saw himself running like the wind, too.

"I'll wait for you, okay?" said Joseph. "By the front gate."

"Okay," Owen said. "See you tomorrow."

He hung up and went to find his mom. He could hear her in the kitchen. When he got to the door, he stopped.

"Holy mackerel," Owen said. "This looks like a disaster area."

The kitchen was a mess. There was flour everywhere. His mother had dough on her sweatshirt. In her hair.

There was even a glob on the side of her nose. But Owen didn't tell her. From the look on her face, he could tell she didn't need any more bad news.

"It *is* a disaster," Mrs. Foote said. "Every time I try to bake bread, it's a disaster."

"Why don't you give up?" said Owen.

"Oh, wonderful, Owen," Mrs. Foote said. She sounded annoyed. "Is that what I've taught you after all these years? If something's hard, you simply give up?"

Owen didn't answer. He knew he'd better get her mind back on the bread. Anywhere but on him.

He walked over to where a loaf was sitting on the counter. It looked okay. It smelled great.

"What's wrong with it?" he said.

"It's as hard as a rock," his mom said. "If you dropped it out a second-story window, you'd kill someone."

She picked it up and let it drop. It landed with an impressive thud.

"Cool," Owen said. "I could shellac it. It would make a great doorstop."

"That's not funny, Owen."

"I'm serious, Mom." He picked it up. It was heavy, all right.

Then he had a better idea. He could use it to catch burglars. If one ever came into his room, Owen would hurl the bread at him.

"Eat this," he'd say. The burglar would think it was a snack. He'd never know what hit him.

"Go ahead and take it," his mom sighed. "Somebody might as well get some use out of it."

"Don't worry, Mom. Someday you'll make bread people can actually eat," Owen said. "Like Anthony Petrocelli's mother. She makes delicious bread. It practically melts in your mouth."

Mrs. Foote's shoulders drooped. "If you're trying to make me feel better, Owen, it's not working."

"Okay, take it easy." Owen grabbed the bread and backed out of the kitchen.

It was a funny thing about grownups, he thought. When a kid couldn't do something, they always said, "Look at so-and-so, he can do it."

Being compared to someone else was supposed to make the kid feel better. Or try harder, or something.

But when a grownup couldn't do something, forget it. Comparing them to someone else made them mad.

Owen carried the bread up to his room. Lydia passed him on the stairs.

"What are you doing with that?" she said.

"Making a doorstop."

Lydia raised her left eyebrow to show Owen he was being ridiculous. "Why are brothers so weird?"

Owen tossed the bread into the air and

caught it. "They inherit it from their sisters," he said.

He didn't wait to see the expression on her face. He went into his bedroom and closed the door. Then he stood in front of the mirror.

"Point for Owen Foote, number nine," he said.

"You're the coolest guy in the whole wide world," the mirror said back.

2.

THE CHESTERFIELD KLUTZ

"If I didn't know better, I'd swear you were being attacked by a mad dog."

Owen's dad stood in the doorway. He was in his bathrobe.

Owen was lying on his back in the living room. Major, his dog, was standing over him. Major's legs straddled Owen's body. He had a corner of Owen's pajamas in his mouth. He was shaking his head back and forth and growling.

Owen was wearing his mother's tall green gardening boots. They came up to his thighs. Just like hip boots.

"I'm pretending I'm a tyrannosaurus and Major's a wolverine," he said. With a quick motion, he grabbed Major around the shoulders and flipped him onto his back. Major's tail started wagging.

"I have to attack him to get him to fight and then he bites my legs," Owen said. He got up and followed his father into the kitchen. "You don't have time to sit around in your pajamas, Dad. Today's soccer, remember?"

His father looked at the clock. "It's six-thirty, Owen. I think we'll make it."

"I told Joseph I'd be there early," Owen said. "He's kind of nervous."

"Tell him not to take it too seriously," Mr. Foote said. "Sports are supposed to be fun. It doesn't matter whether you win or lose."

"It does to kids," Owen said. "Kids want to win. When they don't, they want to kill the kids who did."

"I'm afraid that pretty much sums up human nature," his dad said. He poured water into the coffee maker. "It would be great if people played games for the fun of it, but most of them don't."

"Yeah, it would be great to see a team jumping up and down, yelling, 'We lost, we lost!'"

Owen and his dad laughed.

Joseph was standing by the side of the road when they got to the field. He saw the Footes' car and his whole face smiled. He waved.

"'Bye, Dad." Owen slammed the car door. "Hey, Joseph!"

He and Joseph met halfway. Joseph grabbed his hand and squeezed. Owen squeezed back. Then he remembered where he was. He snatched his hand back and looked around.

In first grade it was okay to hold hands. But not in second grade. At least not where older kids could see you.

And definitely not at soccer practice.

Owen looked around to see if anyone had noticed. But no one had. They were too busy yelling and running around. There were kids in soccer shorts and cleats everywhere.

Some were already kicking balls. Some were

hanging off the nets in the goal. Some of the kids looked huge.

Owen didn't see one familiar face.

His stomach felt as if it was being tickled from the inside. He knew that feeling was called "butterflies." Owen wouldn't mind having butterflies. He liked them.

This felt more like caterpillars.

"What do we do now?" said Joseph.

"We have to find out what team we're on," said Owen. He tried to sound as if he'd done this before. He looked at a crowd of people standing around a long table. Maybe that was where they should go.

Then he heard someone shout, "Owen, over here!"

It was Anthony Petrocelli. He was standing next to the table, waving his hands in the air.

Anthony was in Mrs. LeDuc's class, too. He was always trying to do things faster than everyone else. Like get in line faster. And finish his spelling faster. Even stand up faster.

Usually it drove Owen crazy. But today, he'd never been happier to see anybody.

"Come on!" Owen shouted.

He and Joseph ran over to the table.

"We're all on the same team," Anthony told them. "We're the Aliens."

"Great," Owen said. The name of your team was very important. Aliens was a great name.

"There's a team called the Chipmunks," Anthony said. "I'd die if I was on the Chipmunks."

"I like chipmunks," said Joseph. "They're cute."

Anthony rolled his eyes. "Not for a soccer team."

"Everyone on the Aliens, over here, please." Owen saw a man with bright red hair and a whistle around his neck. "Aliens, let's get going," the man yelled.

A group of kids was crowding around him. Anthony pushed to the front. Owen and Joseph stood at the back. A tall kid elbowed

past Owen and stood right in front of him.

Even on tiptoes, Owen could hardly see what was going on.

"My name is Dave," the man said. "I'm your coach. This is my assistant, Chuck." A short, dark man with a beard smiled and nodded. "The first ten kids to get your name tags, go with Chuck to do push-ups. The rest stay with me for dribbling practice."

Anthony got his tag right away. He went off to do push-ups.

Owen and Joseph were in the dribbling group. So was the tall kid. His tag said WALTER. He was wearing orange socks over his shin guards. His tee shirt said BUTTON YOUR FLY.

Walter grabbed a ball. He bounced it off his left foot, then his right foot. Then off each knee.

Then he headed it to a boy with yellow hair whose tag said JEREMY. Jeremy trapped it, then kicked it back.

Walter caught it on his thigh, spun around,

and kicked it over the goal and into the parking lot.

"Go get it, Walter," Dave yelled. He turned to the rest of them.

"Listen up," he shouted. "If you want to play on my team, you've got to pay attention. I'm not going to waste my time if you're going to fool around."

Owen frowned. His coach at Chesterfield School hadn't yelled like that. None of the kids at Chesterfield School could handle the ball like that, either.

Or kick that hard.

"I don't feel so good," Joseph whispered next to him. His eyes looked big and dark. He put a hand on his stomach.

"He's just showing off," said Owen. He could feel his heart beating. "It's okay."

"Everybody line up," Dave yelled. "I want one line behind this guy." He put his hand on the head of the boy in front of him. He looked down at his tag. "Chris. One line behind Chris."

Everyone pushed in behind Chris. Owen

pulled Joseph toward the back. He definitely didn't want to be first. They got behind Walter.

Walter turned around and looked at Owen.

"How old are you?" he said.

Owen clenched his teeth. He knew Walter didn't really want to know how old he was. Walter was saying he thought Owen was a lot younger than he, Walter, was. Because Owen was small.

"Aren't you supposed to be in Peepers?" Walter asked.

Owen felt his face go hot. Peepers was the new league for kindergartners and first graders. He stared straight ahead.

"Okay, listen up!" Dave yelled. Everyone got quiet. He pointed to a long row of orange cones. "I want you to dribble in and out between the cones all the way to the end and back. Go as fast as you can without knocking any of them down."

He kicked the ball to Chris. Owen watched closely. Chris was pretty good. He wasn't very fast, but he only knocked over two cones.

Some of the other kids were a little better. Some, a little worse.

Walter was great.

He was fast and sure. He moved the ball lightly with the top of his foot. Like in World Cup Soccer, practically. It seemed to go exactly where he wanted it to.

He dribbled down and back without knocking over a single cone.

Watching Walter gave Owen a tight feeling in his throat. As if he wasn't going to be able to do anything right when it was his turn. Then he had a thought. Maybe he'd ended up on the wrong team. Maybe these other kids were third graders.

He thought Walter looked pretty old. Some of the other kids looked older, too. If Dave moved him to a different team, maybe he wouldn't feel so nervous. The kids would be his own age.

And size.

He raised his hand to talk to Dave about it

just as the ball hit him in the stomach. He heard someone laugh.

"Keep your eyes open, Owen," Dave yelled. "It's your turn."

Owen bent and picked up the ball.

"No hands!" Dave yelled. "Rule number one of soccer!"

Owen dropped it as if it was on fire.

He knew about no hands. Only the goalie was allowed to use hands. Everyone knew that.

Owen felt a buzzing in his head as he started to dribble. Left, right, left, right. He moved as carefully as he could.

He knew he was going too slowly. But he had to. If he knocked over a cone, Dave would probably yell at him again.

He didn't think he could take being yelled at anymore the first day.

"Faster, Owen, faster, that's the way. Good job, good job." Dave's voice kept on and on. Owen turned around the last cone and started back. It felt as if the end was a hundred miles away.

He made it. And he only knocked down one cone. "That's it, Owen, good job," Dave said. "Pick up a little speed next time."

Joseph was next. Owen kicked the ball to him and walked slowly to the back of the line. His legs felt weak.

"Get a load of that kid," he heard Walter say.

Owen looked back at the field.

Joseph was halfway down the row. Every cone behind him was lying on its side. It was like a highway, after a car screeches out of control.

He watched Joseph kick. The ball rolled off to one side. Joseph ran after it. When he got up to it, his foot accidentally kicked it again. It rolled farther away.

Walter nudged the kid next to him and laughed. He turned to Owen.

"Is that kid a friend of yours?" he said.

Owen looked at Walter. Then at the boy

standing beside him. He knew other kids were listening. Everyone seemed to be grinning. Everyone seemed to be high above his head.

He felt about one inch tall.

"Not really," he said in a small voice.

"What school does he go to?" said Walter.

"I think Chesterfield."

"Perfect," Walter said. "The Chesterfield Klutz."

A few kids laughed. Walter held his stomach and doubled over. As if it was the funniest thing he'd ever heard.

"The Chesterfield Klutz," he said again.

Owen looked back at Joseph. The coach had his arm around Joseph's shoulders. Joseph's face was bright red. His shorts were pulling up between his thighs.

Owen looked at the ground.

He knew he should tell Walter to cut it out. He knew he should say Joseph was his best friend.

But he couldn't.

If he did, Walter would call him a Chesterfield klutz, too. Then everybody would.

Owen didn't think he could bear to be called that.

So he didn't say anything.

He kept his head down and blinked his eyes, hoping the water in them wouldn't fall out and hit the ground.

3.

ALIENS I OR ALIENS II?

Dave's whistle shrilled.

"All right, everyone over here for push-ups."

Owen got down on the ground. Joseph squatted down next to him. "I was terrible, wasn't I?" he said.

Owen didn't answer. He started doing push-ups to Dave's count. So did Joseph.

After three, Joseph fell face down on the ground. He lay there, breathing heavily.

Owen kept going. His muscles felt as if they were going to explode. He didn't stop until Dave said, "That's enough, Owen, take it easy."

Next, they practiced goal kicks. When Walter kicked the ball, it made the sound Owen loved. That solid sound that meant you'd really connected. The ball flew over the goalie's head and hit the net.

When it was his turn, Owen kicked the ball as hard as he could. But it didn't sound nearly as good. It didn't get past the goalie, either.

Then it was Joseph's turn. He ran forward, took a little hop, and kicked. His foot whipped through the air above the ball.

The ball didn't move. Joseph landed on his bottom.

"The Chesterfield Klutz strikes again," Owen heard Walter say. The yellow-haired kid named Jeremy laughed.

Owen let out his breath in a little burst. All of a sudden, he didn't want to do this anymore. He didn't want to be here or know Joseph or listen to Walter. Or even play soccer.

He wanted this to be over.

Finally, it was. "That's enough for today,"

Dave yelled. "Everybody over here by the goal."

They all sat on the ground and wiped their faces with their tee shirts. They flapped their hands like fans. Chuck passed out cups of water.

Walter drank some, then poured the rest over his head. Jeremy copied him. Then Anthony and a few other kids did, too.

They were laughing and joking around. But not Joseph. And not Owen.

"That was a good first practice," Dave said. "I wanted to see what you know, and you guys look pretty good. We need to practice passing and dribbling. And I saw a lot of you using your hands."

Owen kept his eyes down. He felt as if Dave was looking straight at him.

"It's a hard habit to break, but it'll get you a penalty every time. So starting next practice, if I see anyone using hands, you run one lap around the field."

"No fair!" Owen's brain shouted. He looked at the sweaty faces around him. Chris met his eyes. He gave a tiny shrug.

"We've got practice next Tuesday and Thursday," Dave went on. "Our first game is on Saturday. This is what I've decided to do."

He squatted down to their level. Owen sat up a little straighter. He felt that what was coming next was important.

"We've got a lot of different skill levels here," Dave said. "Some of you are ready to play and some of you could use some extra help. So on Tuesday, I'm going to watch you practice, then divide you into two groups."

Two groups? Owen frowned.

"Aliens I and Aliens II. Kind of like the movies."

Dave tried to make it sound like a joke. But no one laughed. Owen could feel them all listening.

"Aliens I will work with me to get ready for our game on Saturday," said Dave, "and Aliens

II will work with Chuck on sharpening up some skills. It will only be for a few weeks."

A boy with his front teeth missing raised his hand.

"Jason?"

"Will Aliens II ever get to play?" Jason's voice was so low, Owen could barely hear him.

"Sure," Dave said. "No matter which group you're in, we're all the Aliens. I want everyone to understand that, okay?"

"Not okay," Owen wanted to say. Kids don't understand things that don't make sense.

Like making two teams out of one team. And putting the better kids on one team so everyone would know who the worse kids were.

"Okay, then, see you on Tuesday," Dave said.

Owen, Joseph, and Anthony walked to the parking lot.

"Did you see how bad that girl with the ponytail was? She's Aliens II, for sure,"

Anthony said. He leaped in the air and kicked an imaginary ball. "And what about that guy Walter? He's great." He was bouncing on the tips of his toes, talking excitedly.

A car horn honked. A voice called, "Anthony!"

"See you guys on Monday." Anthony sprinted to his car. Owen knew he would brag the whole way home.

He and Joseph walked on. Mr. Hobbs leaned out of his car window and waved.

"Joseph! Owen!"

Joseph got into the front seat. Owen got into the back.

"How'd it go?" Mr. Hobbs asked.

"It was hard," said Joseph. He started telling his dad about knocking down the cones.

Owen looked out the window. They passed a dark blue van. Walter was opening its door. Owen ducked his head.

"Give it time," he heard Mr. Hobbs say. "I'm proud of you for trying, Joseph. It'll get better."

Mr. Hobbs looked at Owen in the rearview mirror. "How about you, Owen? How did you do?"

"Okay." Owen kept his head down. He knew it was rude not to look Mr. Hobbs in the eye. But Mr. Hobbs didn't seem to notice.

Owen stared out the window. He heard Joseph say his name.

He looked up. Joseph was staring at him. "I bet you'll be on Aliens I," Joseph said.

"I don't know," said Owen. He picked at a fingernail. "I was lousy."

"No, you weren't," said Joseph. "You were good."

Owen shrugged. Joseph didn't even know what good was. But Owen did. Next to Walter, he wasn't good. He stank.

He wished Joseph would stop talking. Joseph was just being loyal. The way he always was.

Right now, Owen wished he wouldn't be. He knew he should say something nice to Joseph.

But he couldn't think of a single thing.

It made him feel even worse.

"It's okay if we're not together, Owen." Joseph's eyes were huge pools of sad brown. "Really."

They looked into each other's eyes. It wasn't okay and they both knew it. But they didn't know what to do about it.

The minute Mr. Hobbs's car pulled into his driveway, Owen jumped out. "Thanks for the ride," he said.

He shut the door and walked toward the house.

"Hey, Owen, want to go fishing?" yelled Joseph.

"I can't," Owen said. He walked up the front path.

His mom was on her knees, weeding. She looked up at him.

"Hi, sweetie, how did it go?"

"Terrible." He didn't stop walking. Major came up to him with his tail wagging. Owen went past him and up the front steps.

"Owen?" his mom called. He let the door slam behind him.

He went up to his room and closed the door. He lay down on the bed. He didn't want to talk. He didn't want to think.

All he wanted to do was fall asleep.

When the door opened, he closed his eyes. He hoped whoever it was would go away. Instead, Lydia said, "Hey, how was soccer?"

"Great," he said, "just great."

She leaped onto his bed. "How was Joseph?"

Owen opened his eyes. For a minute he stared at the ceiling. Then he said, "Terrible."

"Was he really?"

"He can't dribble, he can't kick, he can't do anything."

"You knew that, Owen," Lydia said. "He never played before."

There was nothing Owen could say.

"Poor Joseph," said Lydia. "How did you do?"

He could feel Lydia watching him.

"Fine."

"I remember the first time I played in the town league," she said. "It was awful. All the other kids were better than I was."

That was a long time ago, Owen wanted to tell her. Who cares about a long time ago?

"I came home and cried."

Owen picked up a book from his bedside table. He held it up in front of his face, as if he was reading.

Usually, he liked to talk about soccer with Lydia. She was a good player. Sometimes they practiced in the backyard.

But today, all he wanted was for her to go away. He didn't want her to try to make him feel better. It only made him feel worse.

"Boys don't cry about stupid things like soccer," he said. He kept his eyes on the page. "Anyway, it's not like that anymore. Everyone's as good as everyone else."

"That's rude." Lydia stood up. "Joseph's the one who had a hard time. I don't know why you're in such a bad mood."

Owen kept staring at the page. When Lydia

slammed his door, he didn't look up. He simply put the book on his chest and closed his eyes.

Lydia didn't know anything.

He had promised Joseph he'd protect him. But he didn't.

They were best friends. Best friends were supposed to stick together.

Even if it meant being called names. Or being in a group you didn't want to be in. Or being embarrassed by each other.

Even if it ruined the sport you loved more than anything in the world.

Even then.

4.

PARDON MY FAT FOOT

"I don't know if I feel like playing soccer this year."

It was bedtime. Owen was under the covers, waiting for his mom to say good night. She was putting away his clean underwear. When he spoke, she stopped.

"Oh?" She sounded surprised. She came over and sat down on the edge of his bed. She looked at him for a minute. "You never told me about practice."

"It was just practice." Owen blinked. His mom didn't say anything. "It's just that we have practice two times a week this year. Plus a game every Saturday. It'll cut into my leisure time."

Mrs. Foote smiled. "You and your leisure time."

Owen loved his time at home. He never ran out of things to do. About the only thing he loved as much as his leisure time was playing soccer.

He knew his mom knew that.

"What were the other kids like?" she said.

"Just kids." There was a silence. "Some of them were kind of big. They could really kick."

"Is the coach nice?"

"Not as nice as Ray LaBonte."

Ray LaBonte was Owen's coach at Chesterfield School. He never yelled. He liked Owen. Every practice, he rubbed the top of Owen's head and said, "Hey there, big guy."

Thinking about it made Owen feel sad.

"The town league is a big adjustment," his mom said. She smoothed the hair off his forehead. "I suppose you could quit and play again in a few years. But if all the other kids keep on playing, they'll just get better and better. You might never catch up."

"I don't care," Owen said. "They're jerks."

"All of them? Even Anthony and Joseph?"

Owen rolled over on his side and faced the wall. "I don't want to talk about it anymore."

"Maybe you should give it a few more tries," his mom said gently. "Maybe what's bothering you will change."

Owen squeezed his eyes shut. He felt the mattress spring up as his mom stood up. She put her hand on his back and bent down to kiss his cheek.

"It's your decision," she said. "Just don't rush into anything."

She switched off his light. The darkness made him panic. He rolled back to face her. "I'm only eight. This is the biggest decision of my life."

"You're up to it," she said from the doorway. "I have complete faith in you."

Then she was gone.

Owen got up and turned on his night light. Then he climbed back into bed. He pulled his knees up to his chest and curled into a tight ball.

He hadn't meant it when he said he didn't want to talk about it. He meant he didn't think she'd understand. He meant he needed time to straighten it out for himself.

He lay awake for a long time. He was glad his mom felt he was old enough to decide for himself. But just before he fell asleep, he wished he was still young enough that he didn't have to.

Owen walked to school on Monday morning, the way he always did.

The leaves were starting to turn. He heard a male cardinal and saw a flash of red. Then off to the side of the road he spotted something white.

It was a tiny skeleton that looked like a hand. It was only about an inch long. But it had five perfect fingers.

It was eerie-looking.

He could hardly wait to show it to Joseph. It was probably the paw of a squirrel or mouse. But he was going to tell Joseph it was a vampire bat. That would freak him out.

Joseph hated vampire bats.

Owen had found a book about them in the library this summer. It said vampire bats suck the blood of cows at night. First, the bat lands on a cow's back. Then it sinks its teeth into the cow's neck. It can suck out all the blood it wants. The cow never even knows it's there.

Owen had told Joseph this while they were eating cucumbers in Owen's garden.

"The skin's the best part of a cucumber," Owen said. "You feel like a vampire bat."

He held the cucumber in front of his face with both hands. "You sink your teeth into the cow's neck." He took a huge bite in slow motion.

"You hear a *pop!*" Owen chewed slowly. As though he was really enjoying it. "The insides are soft," he said in a spooky voice. "Then you start sucking the blood."

He made loud sucking noises. He bared his teeth as if they were fangs.

Joseph had turned white. He looked at the cucumber in his hand. "I like mine to be peeled," he said. "I think I'll eat this at home."

Owen could hardly wait to show Joseph the skeleton.

He cradled it in his hand all the way to school. But when he got there, Joseph wasn't alone. He was sitting on the front steps with a group of kids.

Owen carefully put the skeleton in his pocket and sat down on the steps.

Anthony was telling them his parents were

going to give him a dollar for every goal he scored this year. Last year, they gave him fifty cents.

"It's no fair," Owen had told his mother. "I have to work a whole week for fifty cents. Anthony gets that much for a single goal."

"I feel sorry for Anthony," his mom said. "Parents like that are tough to live with."

Owen didn't think it sounded tough. He thought it sounded great.

"'Morning, kids." It was Mr. Mahoney, the principal. He stood over them, smiling. "How was soccer this weekend?"

"Great!" Anthony said. "I got two goals but I don't get paid unless it's a real game."

"Our team is called the Aliens," said Joseph.

Mr. Mahoney looked at Owen. "How about you, Owen?"

Mr. Mahoney knew how much Owen loved soccer. Ever since he'd told Owen that he'd played in college, they talked about it all the time.

"It was okay," Owen said.

"Some of the other kids were awesome," said Anthony. "They can kick the ball a mile. They play like high-school kids."

"They're dorks," Owen said. "I bet all they do at their school is play soccer. They think they're so great."

"It takes a lot more than coordination to make a great athlete," Mr. Mahoney said. "Mental attitude is very important. You ask coaches. They'll tell you a lot of Olympic athletes were awkward as kids.

"Isn't that right, Clyde?" Mr. Mahoney put his arm around the shoulders of a boy who had come up beside him.

"Anything you say, Mr. Mahoney."

Clyde Barnes was a seventh grader. He was a computer genius. He had a streak of purple hair and he wore an earring.

He was also the best soccer player in Chesterfield School. Last year, he made the All-Star team in their state. All the kids went to watch him play. They all waved banners that said, CLYDE, CLYDE, CHESTERFIELD'S PRIDE.

Owen still had his banner on his bedroom wall.

"They just joined the town league," Mr. Mahoney told Clyde. "With the big guys."

"I remember that," Clyde said. "I hated soccer that year. Some of those guys were so good, I felt like a wimp."

"*You* hated soccer?" said Owen.

"*You*, a wimp?" said Anthony.

"Everyone's a wimp at the beginning," Clyde said. "I loved it again as soon as I got better."

"Hang in there," Mr. Mahoney told them, "and don't look back unless that's the direction you want to go."

Mr. Mahoney always said things like that. Like he was still in the Marines and they were in his platoon. Lots of times, they didn't know what he meant. But he made them feel grown up.

The bell rang. Everyone started pushing to

get through the front door. Clyde grabbed Owen's arm and held him back.

"Hold on a second, Owen," he said.

Clyde had known Owen since kindergarten when he was Owen's "Big Buddy." That meant he had to show Owen around the school the first few weeks so Owen wouldn't get trampled on by the big kids.

One day, when they came to a dinosaur poster, Owen had stopped.

"I'm going to be a paleontologist when I grow up," he'd told Clyde.

Clyde hadn't even known what a paleontologist was.

"I want to let you in on a little soccer secret," Clyde said now. "I'm telling you because you've got a good head on your shoulders. I wouldn't tell this to just any jerk."

They moved off to one side.

"You and I both know that good sportsmanship is the only way to go, right?"

Owen nodded.

"But every once in a while, you run into a

real dope on the field," Clyde said. "You know the kind I mean."

Owen nodded again. He knew, all right.

"You can only use what I'm about to show you in dire emergencies, okay?"

Owen didn't know what "dire" meant, but he'd look it up later. "Sure," he said.

"Say you're running side by side with some guy who's really been bugging you. He's got the ball."

He stood right next to Owen. They were facing the door. Clyde was on Owen's right side. He grabbed Owen's arm and started walking.

"What you do is, reach over with the heel of your inside foot." He moved his left foot in front of Owen's right foot. "You let it get in the way for a second. Then you yank it back."

He pulled his foot from in front of Owen's. Owen stumbled and almost fell. Clyde's arm kept him on his feet.

"Oh, I'm so sorry," Clyde said in a polite voice. "Did my fat foot get in your way?"

"Is that legal?"

"Being a klutz? Sure." Clyde ran his hand through his purple streak. "You're a smart kid, Owen, and you're a nice kid, too. But sometimes, being a nice kid is tough on a guy, you know what I mean?"

All Owen could do was nod.

"I know you won't use it unless you really have to, right?"

"Right," Owen said. "Thanks."

When he got to his classroom, Mrs. LeDuc was taking attendance. Owen slid into his seat.

"What did Clyde want?" Anthony whispered from across the aisle. His eyes were practically falling out of his head.

"He needed a few soccer tips," Owen said.

"Yeah, right."

"Owen, do you have something you'd like to share with the rest of the class?" Mrs. LeDuc called from the front of the room.

"No, Mrs. LeDuc," Owen said. He bent over and started looking through his desk.

He wasn't about to share this secret. It was between him and Clyde. Chesterfield's Pride had picked him, Owen, to give a personal tip to.

And it felt good.

Very good.

5.

SOMEONE TO HANG ON TO

Owen was watching his feet. His new black cleats had bright green stripes down the side. In the store he thought maybe they glowed in the dark. When he got home, he wore them into the closet. They didn't.

He was walking as slowly as he could. But he was still getting closer and closer to practice.

Not practice. Today wasn't going to be practice. It was going to be more like a tryout, Owen thought. He didn't feel as if he was old enough to try out. But he couldn't say that to Anthony. Anthony probably thought tryouts were great.

And he didn't have to ask Joseph. Joseph was walking even more slowly than Owen.

"Come on, you guys," Anthony said. He was bouncing around in the road, kicking stones into the gutter. "We're going to be late."

When they got to the field, Dave said they were going to practice passing. That made Owen feel a little better. He was good at passing. Last year, Ray LaBonte gave him a certificate at the end of the year that said BEST PASSER.

Dave started pairing them up. He put his hand on Owen's shoulder. "Okay, Owen, let's see." He looked around. "Walter," he called, "why don't you and Owen work together."

"Great," Walter said under his breath. But loud enough for Owen to hear. He grabbed a ball and started dribbling. Owen had to run to keep up.

Then, without a word, Walter kicked the ball with the outside of his foot. It shot toward Owen. Owen lunged for it, but it flew past him. He ran after it and kicked it back. It rolled a few feet and stopped.

Walter crouched down and beckoned with his hands. "Come on, a little bit farther, that's the way. You can do it."

As if it was a baby trying to walk.

If anyone else had done that, it would have sounded like a joke. Owen would have laughed.

With Walter, it wasn't funny.

"Cut it out," Owen said.

"Cut what out?" said Walter. "I don't want the little Peeper to get hurt."

He started kicking to Owen very gently. "Is that too hard for you?" he kept saying.

Owen didn't know what to do. He was mad at himself for being nervous, mad that he was so small, mad that Walter was so good.

If he told Dave, he knew Walter would call him a tattletale. He'd treat him even more like a baby.

So he kept playing, with the pressure building up inside him.

Having Joseph nearby only made it worse.

Whenever Joseph made a mistake, Walter

said, "The Chesterfield Klutz strikes again," in a deep voice like a sports announcer.

When it was time to practice dribbling, Owen went and stood as far away from Walter as he could. Dave put him in a group with Chris, Jason, and the girl with the ponytail. Her name was Jemma.

They had to dribble the ball down the field, around a cone, and back. Then pass to the next person in line.

Chris went first. He dribbled around the cone, came back, and passed to Owen. Owen trapped the ball and dribbled around the cone and back. He passed to Jemma and went to the end of the line.

"That was good," Chris said.

"Thanks," said Owen. They watched Jemma. She was kind of slow, but she wasn't so bad. No one laughed at her.

They were all just about the same, Owen realized. It felt nice.

He looked for Joseph.

Joseph was in a group near the goal. It was

his turn to kick. Owen heard someone yell, "Hey, klutz, catch!"

He saw Walter punt the ball into the air. He saw Joseph turn around.

Owen knew what was going to happen. He wanted to shout, to warn Joseph. To make Walter stop.

Anything. But it was too late.

Joseph should have stopped the ball with his body, but he didn't know how.

So he reached out and caught it.

Dave's whistle blasted. "No hands, Joseph! Sorry, but I warned you. Once around the field."

"No fair!" The words burst out of Owen like a rocket. Now Joseph would get mad. He and Owen would tell Dave what Walter had been doing. He'd make Walter stop.

But Joseph didn't get mad. He started running.

Owen couldn't believe it. He whirled around to look for Dave. But he was already walking down the field, talking to Chuck.

Walter was at the back of his line, laughing.

It was over, and there was nothing Owen could do about it. The rest of practice passed in a blur. He didn't know who he wanted to yell at more. Walter or Dave.

Or Joseph.

When practice was over, he left the field as fast as he could.

"Hey, Owen, wait!" Joseph ran up behind him. "Slow down, would you?"

Owen kept walking. He kept his eyes on the street.

For a few minutes they didn't talk. Then Joseph said, "Remember how you told me not to step too hard on the ball when I trap it? Well, I forgot. One time I fell on my face. Jeremy said he'd lend me his nose guard next time."

Owen stopped so fast, Joseph bumped into him. His chest was still heaving up and down from his run around the field.

"There's no such thing as a nose guard," Owen said. His voice was tight.

"I know that," said Joseph. He looked puzzled. "It was a joke."

"Real funny," Owen said. They looked at each other without saying a word.

Owen started walking again. Then he stopped. "Why did you run when Walter threw you the ball? Why didn't you tell Dave?"

"It's a rule, Owen. I used my hands," Joseph said.

"Walter did it on purpose," Owen said.

"I know that."

"Then why didn't you get mad at him? Why didn't you do something?"

Joseph looked at him. His shoulders sagged.

"Like what?" he said.

Owen saw his huge eyes. His sweaty face.

"Like what," was right.

Joseph wasn't Walter. He was Joseph.

And Owen wasn't mad at him. He was mad because something unfair was happening and he didn't know how to stop it.

His anger oozed out of him. He shook his

head back and forth. "I wish I had my balloon machine. That would show him."

"Yeah." Joseph smiled for the first time. "It sure would."

The balloon machine was an idea Owen had invented in first grade. It was designed to get rid of enemies.

The way it worked was, when a person walked into it, you slammed a door, then pushed a button. When the person was turned into a balloon, a hole opened in the roof and the balloon floated out.

Then you popped it.

The machine was a wonderful idea, but Owen had never figured out how to build one.

"Look. Walter's a balloon." He nudged Joseph. They both stared up at the sky as if there really was a huge, fat Walter balloon floating there.

Owen held up an imaginary pin.

"Good-bye, Walter," Joseph said. He saluted.

Owen jabbed the air. "POP!"

They looked up at the empty sky. No more Walter. It gave Owen a happy feeling. He threw his arm around Joseph's shoulders.

"You know what?" he said.

"What?"

"I went down to the pond with my dad this weekend. You could hear the fish jumping a mile away. It sounded like raccoons doing cannonballs."

Joseph laughed. "Cannonballs" was almost like their secret code word. They both loved doing cannonballs.

All summer long they practiced running to the tip of the diving board. Hurling themselves into the air with their arms wrapped around their knees.

Seeing who could make the loudest sound when they hit the water.

This weekend when Owen heard the fish, he imagined it was raccoons. He could see their striped tails flying out behind them. He could hear them as they hit the water, *whap! whap! whap!*

He knew Joseph could hear it, too.

They staggered down the road together, weaving from side to side. Joseph had to lean down and Owen had to stand on tiptoe. But they kept their arms around each other's shoulders.

It felt good, having someone to hang on to.

6.

I AM SOMEBODY

"Hello?"

"May I please speak to Dave?"

"This is Dave."

"It's Owen Foote. From soccer."

"Yes, Owen, how are you doing?"

"Good."

"What can I do for you?" said Dave.

Owen gripped the phone tighter. He'd known exactly what he wanted to say until he heard Dave's voice. Now there was a loud pounding in his ears. His throat felt like the desert.

He swallowed. "It's about the groups. I

don't care which group I'm in, but I want to be with Joseph. I talked him into playing soccer. He's my best friend, and if he gets into a different group than I do, he's going to think we're not the same anymore and that's going to make him feel terrible."

"But I told you, Owen, it doesn't matter which group you're in," Dave said. "We're all the Aliens. Remember?"

"I know you said that, but that's not how kids feel," Owen said. "If one group is called number one and the other group is number two, everyone knows the good kids are in number one."

Dave was quiet. Owen wished he'd say something.

"I see," Dave said finally. "So the bad kids are in number two, is that it?"

"Yes." Relief lit up Owen's voice.

"I hear you, Owen," Dave said. "I guess I should have thought it through a little bit more. I'll take care of it."

"Thanks," said Owen. "Thanks a lot."

"Thank *you*," said Dave. "I really appreciate your call."

"You're welcome," Owen said. "See you tomorrow."

"See you tomorrow."

•

"Everyone sit down on the ground, please." Dave was standing near the goal. He was holding his clipboard. "I have something important to say."

The kids scurried like crabs to sit down next to someone they knew. "Something important" meant groups. Chris sat next to Owen and held his hand against his chest. His fingers were crossed.

"It has been brought to my attention that I made a major, dumb mistake last Saturday."

Everyone looked surprised. It wasn't every day that a grownup said he'd made a mistake.

Especially a major, dumb mistake.

Owen could feel his ears burning. He hadn't said that. He wouldn't dare say that.

"Everyone who wants to be in Aliens II, raise your hand," said Dave.

They all looked at one another. Not a hand went up.

"See? That's what I mean." Dave paced back and forth in front of them. "I thought dividing us up into two groups would help make us a stronger team. But it didn't, did it?"

No one said anything, but Owen saw heads shake back and forth.

"So forget about my dumb idea," said Dave. "No groups. We're the Aliens. Period. Everyone's the same, everyone gets to play. Okay?"

"Okay," a few voices said. They sounded happy. They loved hearing Dave say dumb. They loved being one team.

"You guys have got to help me out," Dave said. "If I do something you don't like, you've got to speak up. I can play soccer, but I can't read minds. So if you have something to say, you've got to say it, okay?"

"Okay."

"Who are we?"

"The Aliens."

"Who?" He cupped his hand around his ear. "I can't hear you."

"The Aliens!" everyone shouted.

"Right," said Dave. "Now, let's get going. Today we're going to have a scrimmage. Come get an armband."

All the kids scrambled to their feet. Joseph was smiling. So were Chris and Jason. So was everyone, Owen realized, looking around.

Owen, Joseph, and Chris got orange bands. Owen saw Walter put a green band on his arm.

Good, he thought. He wouldn't have to pass to Walter. He'd just have to keep away from him.

"Mike, you want to be goalie?" Dave said to a small, wiry boy.

"Not really," Mike said.

Owen didn't blame him. No one wanted to be goalie. Every time the other team scored, your team blamed you just a little bit, if you were goalie. They weren't supposed to, but they did.

"Okay." Dave looked around. "Joseph. How about you?"

Joseph looked surprised. Then he shrugged. "Okay."

"Great," said Dave. "Chuck will tell you what to do."

Dave looked at his clipboard. "Okay, let me see. Mike, you can play defense. Jemma and Anthony, fullbacks. Owen . . ."

"Yes?"

"Right halfback."

Owen grinned. Halfback was his favorite position. He had to cover the entire side of the field from one end to the other. It meant a lot of running. Owen loved it.

Dave tossed a coin. The green team got the ball. They started passing.

"*To* someone," Owen heard Dave yell.

"Pick a player!" called Chuck.

That meant everyone was supposed to pick a player on the other team and stay with him. Owen looked around. Walter was coming straight at him. He had the ball.

Owen ran forward and tried to block him. Walter kicked the ball to the right and ran around him. Owen turned and caught up to him.

Walter jabbed him with his elbow. Owen kept running. Walter jabbed him again. Hard. "Out of the way, Peeper."

That did it.

Owen slipped his foot out to the side. His heel stopped for a fraction of a second in front of Walter's foot.

Then he pulled it back.

Walter went down. He covered his head with his arms and rolled off to one side. Owen got the ball and passed to Chris. Chris raced toward the goal.

Owen stopped and turned around. Walter was on his feet, brushing off his knees. They were covered with grass stains.

Owen walked back and stood in front of him. Walter was bigger than Owen was, and he was mad. But Owen wasn't scared.

The scariest thing had been feeling afraid. And he wasn't afraid anymore.

"You did that on purpose," Walter said. He was glaring at Owen. His hands were clenched into fists at his sides.

"You deserved it," said Owen. "You got Joseph into trouble. You call everybody names. You laugh at everyone and make fun of them and think you're so great."

"So?"

"So, we're all on the same team," Owen said. "If you're so great, why don't you help other people?"

"Maybe I don't feel like it," said Walter.

"If Joseph is a Chesterfield Klutz, then so am I," Owen said. "He's my best friend."

"Okay, okay, you don't have to make such a big deal of it." Walter sounded nervous. He was looking over Owen's shoulder.

"Is there some trouble here?" It was Dave.

Owen and Walter looked at each other.

"No," they said at the same time.

"Are you okay?" Dave said to Walter.

"Yeah," Walter said. "I must have tripped."

"Okay, then let's get going."

Owen ran back to his position. He felt as if he could run up and down the field forever and not get tired.

As fast as the wind.

•

The orange and green teams tied, 2–2.

"You look great," Dave told them while they drank water. "I think we'll have a good game on Saturday. Are you still willing to play goalie, Joseph?"

"Sure," Joseph said. Sweat was dripping down his face. He looked happy. "I like it. You don't have to run around as much."

Everyone laughed.

"See you on Saturday. Be here at seven-thirty—half an hour before the game," Dave said.

Chris came over and grabbed Owen's arm. "That was great, what you did to Walter. He's a dope."

"It served him right." Jemma had come up next to Chris. "He kept pulling my hair. He's mean."

"Yeah." This was Jason. "He kept kicking me in the bottom."

"Well, he won't anymore," said Joseph. He looked past Owen and raised his voice. "He can't pick on a whole team, right? Not if we stick together."

Out of the corner of his eye, Owen saw Walter walk by. He was looking straight ahead. He had heard every word.

Owen and Joseph slapped hands.

"That wasn't an accident, was it?" said Anthony on the way home.

Owen shrugged. "Not really."

"Cool," Anthony said. Owen could tell he was impressed. "I didn't know you could do that."

Owen hadn't known either. But it was funny, he thought. You never knew what you could do until you tried.

He didn't like being mean, but he was proud he had finally stood up for himself. And for all the other kids Walter had bullied.

He knew he was Somebody again.

And now Walter knew it, too.

7.

"THE ALIENS HAVE LANDED"

The Aliens won their first game, 1–0.

The Comets were good. But the Aliens were better.

Everyone got to play. Owen played halfback again. Walter was defense. He kept getting the ball away from the other team and passing it.

During the second half Joseph was goalie. He blocked three attempts.

Then, at the last minute, Anthony scored. The moment the ball shot past the Comet goalie, the Aliens all started jumping up and down. Anthony kept leaping up and down.

"One dollar!" he shouted. "One whole dollar!"

When the game was over, the Aliens made a circle around Dave. They put their arms around one another's shoulders. "Two, four, six, eight! Who do we appreciate? Comets, Comets, yea-a-a-ah!"

The Comets cheered for the Aliens. Then the two teams lined up, single file, facing each other. The two lines walked past each other, slapping palms. "Good game, good game," they all said.

It looked like two centipedes slapping five.

Owen's dad came up to him. "How would you like to invite a few friends for a barbecue?"

"Sure," Owen said. He asked Joseph and Anthony and Chris and Jason and Jemma.

They raced all the way to the Footes' house. Owen's mom gave them each a soda. They went into the backyard and sat down under a tree.

"Want to see something cool?" said Chris. "It's called the dribble can. My brother learned it in camp."

He opened his can of soda. "First, you have to drink a bit." He sipped and turned to Owen. "Do you have a nail?"

"Sure." Owen ran into the garage and took a nail from his dad's workbench. He ran back and gave it to Chris.

"Now watch." Chris held the can in one hand. He pressed the nail into the side of the can right under the opening.

It made a tiny hole.

Chris licked the soda that leaked out.

"Here's what you do. You offer someone a drink of your soda. When they take a drink"—he tilted the can as if he were drinking—"it pours out all over their clothes."

They watched. Instead of coming out through the top, the soda dribbled out the small opening and onto the grass.

"Cool!" Owen said.

"Can I try?" said Joseph. Chris gave him the can.

That's when Mr. Foote walked over to them.

"Lunch in five minutes, kids." He wiped his forehead. "Anybody have a cold drink for a hot cook?"

Owen looked at Joseph. Joseph looked at Owen.

Then Joseph held up the can. "You can have some of mine, Mr. Foote."

Nobody else said a word.

"Thank you, Joseph," Mr. Foote said. "I knew I could count on you."

He took the can and held it up to his mouth.

He tilted his head back.

Soda dribbled out the hole and made a long wet streak down the front of his shirt.

Mr. Foote jumped back. He held the can away from him with a puzzled expression on his face. He looked at his shirt.

Owen gave a yelp. Chris and Jemma clapped their hands over their mouths. Anthony and Jason started rolling around on the grass.

Joseph looked nervous.

For a second, Mr. Foote didn't do anything. He looked at Owen and the kids trying not to laugh and the others rolling on the ground. Then he looked at Joseph and winked.

"Honey, call 911!" he yelled over his shoulder toward the house. "The Aliens have landed!"

"Hip, hip, hooray!" the Aliens shouted.

8.

"YOU VILL NEVER ESCAPE!"

The minute they walked into the garage after school, Owen smelled it.

"Be careful," he said to Joseph. "My mom might be in a really bad mood."

"Maybe I better come over tomorrow," Joseph said. He wanted to practice goal kicks with Owen, but not that much. He was a little afraid of Mrs. Foote, even when she was in a good mood.

"It's okay," said Owen. "I'll go first."

He opened the kitchen door a crack. "Hi, Mom. How's it going?"

"Owen!" Mrs. Foote flung open the door.

She had flour in her hair and a huge smile on her face. "I did it. I actually made bread you can eat."

"It's safe," Owen said to Joseph. They followed Owen's mom into the kitchen. The smell of bread filled every corner of the room. It smelled great.

Joseph sniffed the air. He looked like Major when food was on the counter.

"That smells delicious, Mrs. Foote," he said.

"It *is* delicious, Joseph. I can't believe it." She was bustling around the kitchen like a small tornado. She kept peering through the glass door of the oven.

"It was the yeast, that's what it was. I finally bought myself a thermometer. I'd been using water that was too cold all along, can you believe it?"

"Calm down, Mom. Don't have a conniption fit." Owen rolled his eyes at Joseph. It was a little embarrassing, having a mother who went cuckoo pots about a loaf of bread.

But Joseph wasn't looking at him. He was

watching Mrs. Foote. Hanging on her every word. When it came to food, Joseph understood craziness.

He watched her take the butter out of the refrigerator. Then the jam. He looked every bit as happy as she did.

The timer went off.

"You boys sit down right here," she said. She put her hand on the oven door. "And now, for the first time ever, Joan Foote's World-Famous, It-Only-Took-Two-Years-To-Get-It-Right Bread."

She opened the door with a flourish. The minute Owen saw the pale brown loaf, he remembered.

"Wait a minute, Mom." He grabbed Joseph's arm to stop him from sitting down. "Come upstairs first, Joseph. There's something I have to show you."

"Now?" said Joseph. He didn't sound happy.

"You can't go now, Owen," Mrs. Foote said. "You have to be the first to try it."

"This is really important, Mom." He didn't let go of Joseph's arm. "Anyway, aren't you supposed to let it cool off for a few minutes? Mrs. Petrocelli always does."

Mrs. Foote frowned. "Maybe you're right."

"I'd sure hate to see you ruin it." Owen pulled Joseph firmly toward the stairs. Joseph looked longingly at the bread.

Mrs. Foote was deep into her cookbook. "You're absolutely right, Owen. It says here you have to let it rest for fifteen minutes." She looked at Joseph. "Go ahead, Joseph. I'll call you when it's time."

Owen kept his hand on Joseph's arm all the way up the stairs. He slammed his bedroom door behind them and pulled Joseph over to his desk.

"More bread?" said Joseph. "You're not allowed to have food in your room."

"It's not food," said Owen. "It's my safe."

He rapped the loaf with his knuckles. It sounded as if he was knocking on wood.

"Remember the catalog with the hiding place that looked like dog poop? The one for car keys? That's what this is. I shellacked it and my dad cut it with his saw."

He pulled the two halves of the bread apart. Inside was a small, hollowed-out cavity. Owen took a wad of paper out of it.

"You won't believe your eyes," he promised Joseph.

He unwrapped the paper carefully and held up the tiny skeleton hand.

"Wow," Joseph said. His voice sounded as if he was afraid the hand might move. "What do you think it is?"

"A vampire bat. I'm sure of it."

Joseph looked at Owen. Then he looked at the hand. For just a second, he hesitated. Then he picked up the hand and held it between two fingers.

"I vant to suck your blood," he said in a voice like Dracula's. He moved the skeleton toward Owen's neck. "You von't feel a thing."

Owen felt the bone scrape his skin. He shrieked and rolled onto the floor.

Joseph kept coming. "You vill never escape. Never!"

Owen shrieked again. But this time, it wasn't a shriek of terror.

It was a shriek of joy.